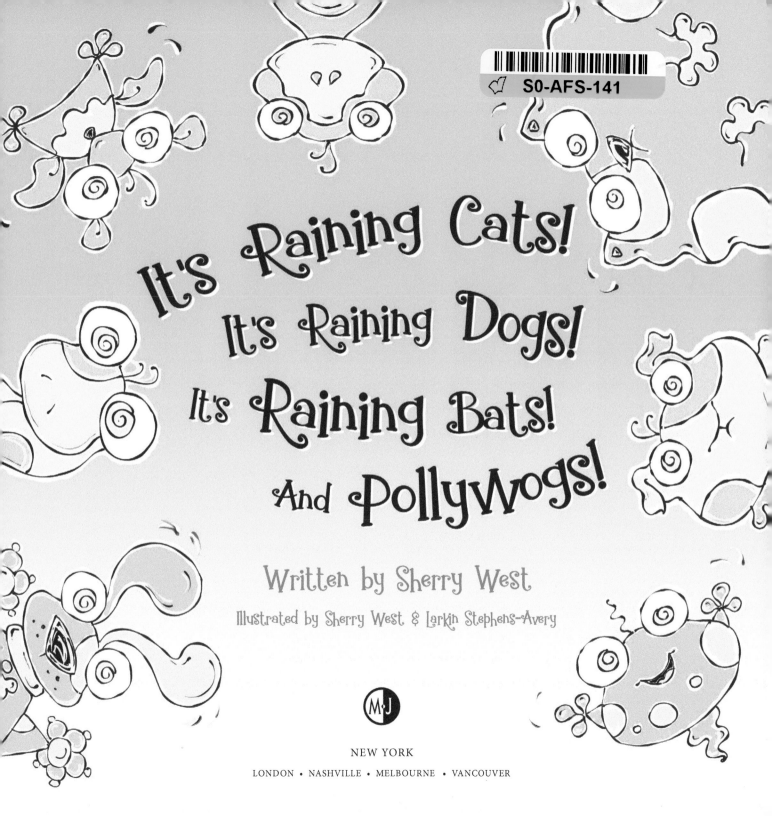

It's Raining Cats! It's Raining Dogs! It's Raining Bats! And Pollywogs!

Written by Sherry West

Illustrated by Sherry West & Larkin Stephens-Avery

M·J

NEW YORK

LONDON · NASHVILLE · MELBOURNE · VANCOUVER

It's Raining Cats, It's Raining Dogs! It's Raining Bats and Pollywogs!

Published in New York, New York, by Morgan James Publishing. Morgan James is a trademark of Morgan James, LLC. www.MorganJamesPublishing.com

The Morgan James Speakers Group can bring authors to your live event. For more information or to book an event visit The Morgan James Speakers Group at www.TheMorganJamesSpeakersGroup.com.

ISBN 9781642793918 paperback
ISBN 9781642793925 eBook
Library of Congress Control Number: 2018914298

Cover and Interior Design by:
Christopher Kirk
www.GFSstudio.com

In an effort to support local communities, raise awareness and funds, Morgan James Publishing donates a percentage of all book sales for the life of each book to Habitat for Humanity Peninsula and Greater Williamsburg.

Get involved today! Visit www.MorganJamesBuilds.com

It's raining **Cats**!

It's raining **Dogs**!

It's raining **Bats**!

And **Pollywogs**!

Here's a **Zebra**,

there's a **Moose**,

The **Zoo** up there

is turning **loose**.

Every **Animal**
that it can **rain**,
And then some more
come down **again**!

They're raining **high**,
they're raining **low**,

They're raining **fast**,
they're raining **slow**!

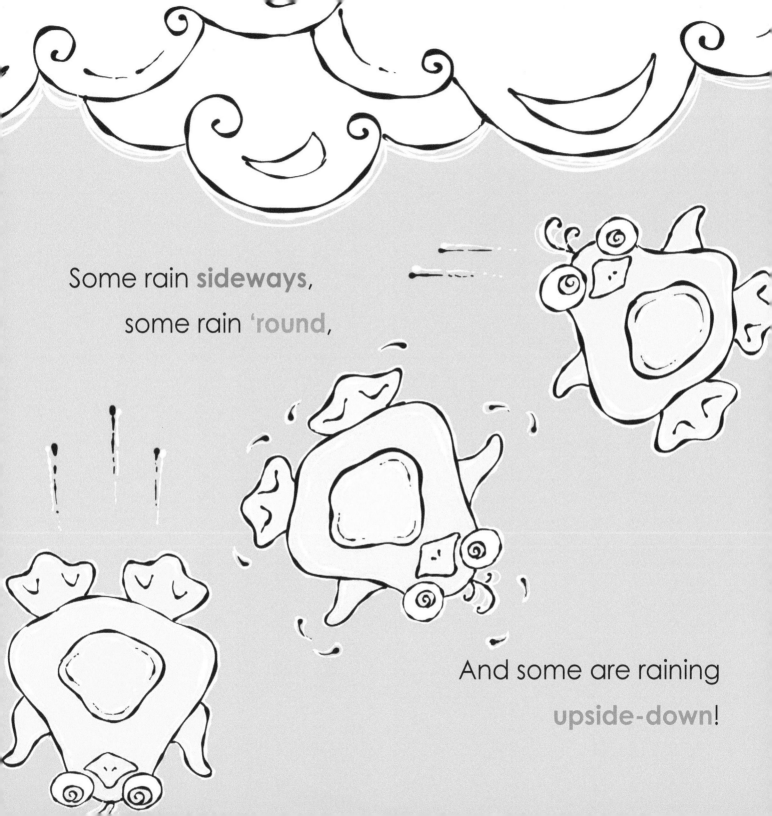

Some rain **sideways**,
some rain **'round**,

And some are raining

upside-down!

Then rained down
some fluffy **Sheep** –

They softly landed
in a **heap**.

One fell in my coffee **mug**.

Ewww, gross! It's a **Slug**!

Some came down
that weren't too **big**.
It was a herd of
Guinea Pig.

Uh-oh, look,
there's a **Snake** –

I think he landed
in a **lake**.

The heavens opened –
down they **sent**

One quite
noisy **Elephant**.

Up above

I heard a **fuss**,

In came a grumpy

Hippopotamus!

I'm pretty sure it's been a while

Since I've seen a Crocodile.

Wet and slimy,
with a **Skwoosh!** –
Down plopped a
perplexed Octopus.

Look! Here come
the **Pollywogs**!

Wait, nope.

Those are **Frogs**.

I'm gonna say
I have to laugh,

'Cause that is one
confused Giraffe.

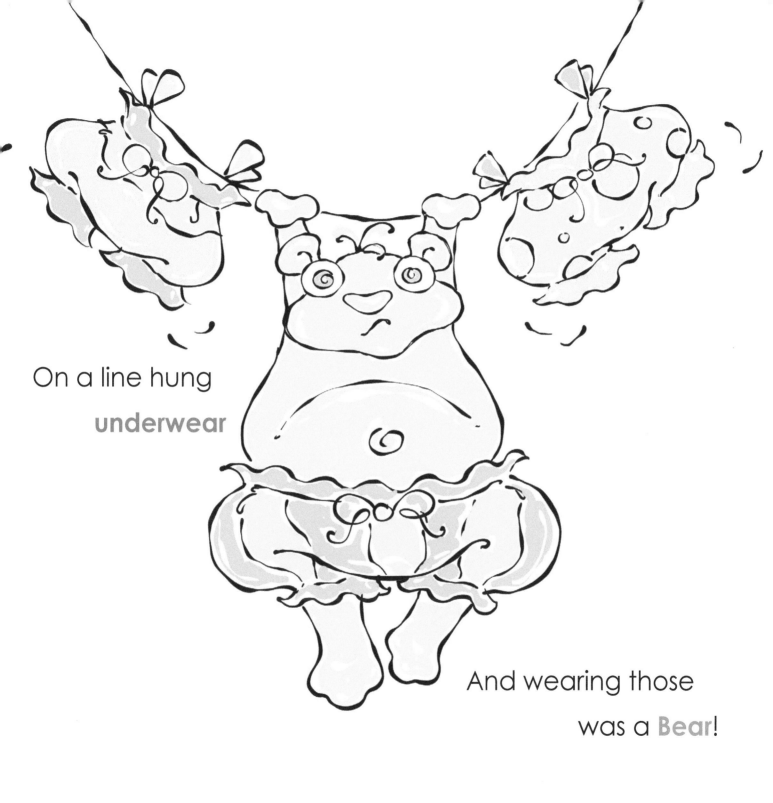

On a line hung

underwear

And wearing those

was a Bear!

The **Mice** came down

with a **Squeak**!

They'll be raining

'til next **week**.

A **Pig** touched
down with a **Splat!**

(I didn't know they rained like that.)

Oh, my, there's
a **Kangaroo**!

Wait, not just one,
I think, but **two**!

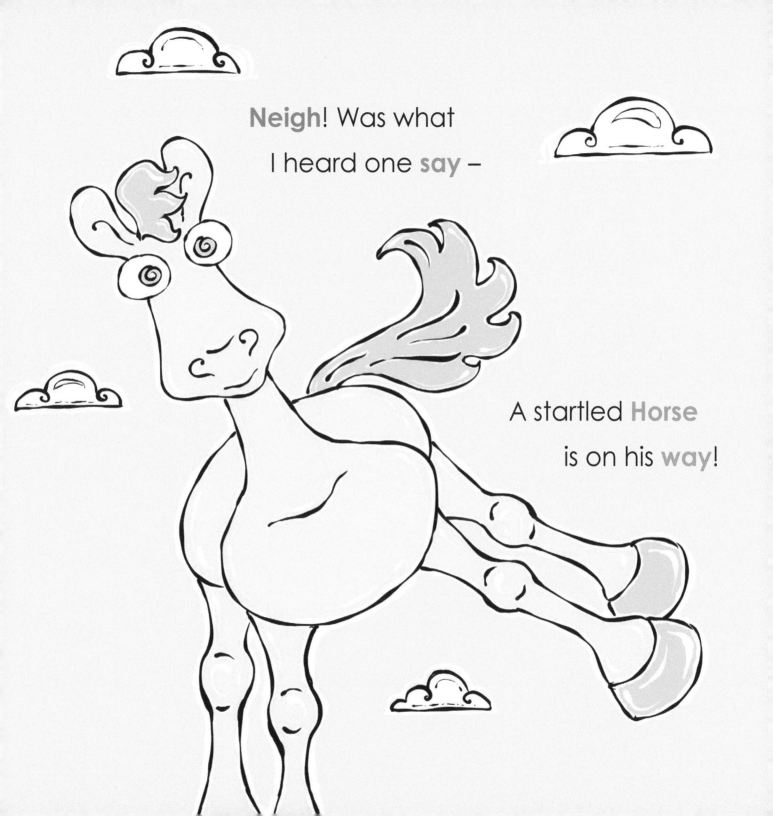

Oh, my goodness,
take a gander
At that spotted
Salamander.

We have to duck
and run for **cover** –

While **Chickens** cluck
and near us **hover**.

They're raining fast
all over **town** –

I wonder what else
is coming **down**?

About the Author and Illustrators

Sherry West has been married for almost 20 years, teaches her three children (ages 3 to 17) at home, and has just way too many cats. She has her bachelor's degree in English, Creative Writing; has taught English as a Second Language for many years to an amazing amount of completely delightful international students; and has written curriculum for a large international educational company as well as for her own classrooms and students. Her award-winning poetry and articles have been published online and in print. She was a member of Teachers of English to Speakers of Other Languages and the Academy of American Poets. Sherry currently resides in Peru, Indiana.

Larkin Stephens-Avery knew she wanted to create art since she was a little girl. She struggled in the normal classroom setting because of her dyslexia but flourished in the art room. She is currently pursuing a major in Fine Arts and a minor in Environmental and Earth Science at Indiana University. She loves spending time with her family and friends and hanging out with her six pet chickens.

CPSIA information can be obtained
at www.ICGtesting.com
Printed in the USA
LVHW071150050819
626532LV00003B/4/P